Walt Disney's MICKEY
and the Beanstalk

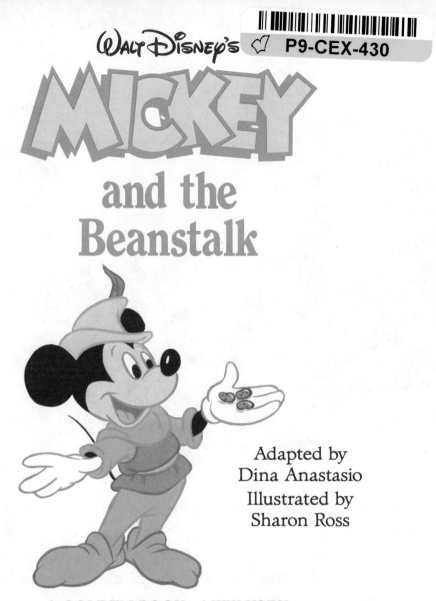

Adapted by
Dina Anastasio
Illustrated by
Sharon Ross

A GOLDEN BOOK • NEW YORK
Western Publishing Company, Inc., Racine, Wisconsin 53404

Far, far away, where the trees were greener than the prettiest green and the sky was bluer than the brightest blue, there was a place called Happy Valley. In Happy Valley the brooks babbled, the birds sang, and everyone smiled all day long.

The farmers whistled and hummed as they did their chores. Children sang as they skipped to school. In Happy Valley every day was a happy day.

High on a hill, overlooking Happy Valley, stood a magnificent castle. In the castle was the Golden Harp, who sang all day and cast a magic spell of happiness over the land.

But one day a terrible thing happened in Happy Valley. Someone stole the Golden Harp from the castle, and the magic spell of happiness was gone.

The birds stopped singing. The brooks stopped
babbling. The crops stopped growing. The cows stopped
giving milk. And all the people of Happy Valley grew sad
and hungry.

"We must do something," said Farmer Donald.
"We'll starve if we don't," added Farmer Goofy.
"I know!" said Farmer Mickey. "I'll sell Bossy the cow and buy some food."

Mickey took the cow into town and sold her. When he returned, he said, "I have sold Bossy for three wonderful beans."

"Three beans!" cried Donald and Goofy. "We can't live on three beans!" Donald threw the beans on the floor in disgust.

"But...but...they are magic beans," said Mickey as he sadly watched the beans roll through a crack in the floor.

But Goofy and Donald didn't pay any attention to what Mickey was saying. They were too tired and hungry to listen.

During the night a moonbeam shone through the window and through the crack in the floor onto the beans.

The beans sprouted and began to grow. They grew into a stalk that lifted the house. The beanstalk climbed all the way up to the sky.

In the morning the hungry farmers woke up and looked out the window.

To their surprise Happy Valley was gone! All they could see from their window was a tremendous castle.

"Let's go!" said Mickey. "Whoever lives in that big castle must have plenty of food to share!"

Mickey, Donald, and Goofy climbed up to the top of the castle stairs and crawled under the front door. On an enormous table they saw huge platters of food. Mammoth pitchers of fresh cold milk waited for them. The farmers quickly climbed up a table leg and ate, drank, and laughed merrily.

As they were finishing their meal a tiny voice called out to them.

"Who's that?" asked Mickey.

"It came from in there," said Donald, pointing to a box that was on the table.

Mickey, Donald, and Goofy moved closer to the box. "Who are you?" they asked.

"It is I, the Golden Harp," said a soft voice. "A giant kidnapped me and brought me here to his castle to sing for him."

The farmers were very frightened to hear that the castle belonged to a giant. They were so frightened that they almost ran away.

"Wait!" cried Mickey suddenly. "We can't leave without the Golden Harp."

"You're right," said Goofy bravely. "We have to rescue her and save Happy Valley!"

Just then they heard loud footsteps. Everything in the room was shaking as the footsteps came closer and closer.

"You must hide!" cried the Golden Harp.

Mickey, Donald, and Goofy ran as quickly as they could to hide from the evil giant.

The giant stomped over to the table and picked up
a giant sandwich in his giant hand. He was just about
to take a bite when he noticed that the sandwich
was moving.

"There's a mouse in my sandwich!" roared the giant.

"Oh, I'm sorry," said Mickey. "I had no idea this was
your sandwich." He jumped from the sandwich to the
giant's shirt and then slid down the giant's leg.

"Run!" shouted Mickey to Donald and Goofy.
The giant was furious. He chased the three farmers
around the room until they were cornered. The giant
reached down to scoop them up in his hand—but he
missed Mickey!

The great big giant put the tiny little farmers into the box with the Golden Harp. He locked the box and slipped the key into his great big pocket. Then he sat down in a chair to take a nap.

Mickey waited in his hiding place behind the pitcher. When the giant finally fell asleep, Mickey tiptoed over to the box and knocked.

"The key," whispered the Golden Harp. "Get the key out of his pocket."

Mickey hurried over to the sleeping giant. Very slowly and carefully he pulled the key out of the giant's pocket.

The giant mumbled something and stirred, but he did not wake up.

Mickey tiptoed back to the box and unlocked it.
Goofy and Donald climbed out and then quickly lifted
out the Golden Harp. The four were very quiet as they
made their way to the front door.

Just as they were sneaking past the giant, he opened
one eye and let out a giant roar.

Goofy and Donald ran with the Golden Harp in their arms. Mickey realized the giant would catch them unless he could do something to distract him.

"You can't catch me!" Mickey taunted. The angry giant ran toward Mickey, who dived under a rug. "Over here!" Mickey said, but the giant was not fast enough to catch Mickey.

Mickey ran toward an open window. "So long!" he shouted as he jumped outside.

Mickey ran to the beanstalk with the giant following close behind. He jumped on the beanstalk and slid down in a flash.

Donald and Goofy grabbed a saw and cut down the beanstalk in the nick of time. The giant fell and crashed through the ground, all the way to the center of the earth.

The farmers took the Golden Harp back to her castle to sing, and from that time on, Happy Valley was happy once again. And happiest of all were the three brave farmers—Mickey, Donald, and Goofy!